P9-CLR-202

BEAR IN A SQUARE

Written by Stella Blackstone • Illustrated by Debbie Harter

Narrated by Henry Strozier

Barefoot Books

step inside a story

Find the bear
in the square.

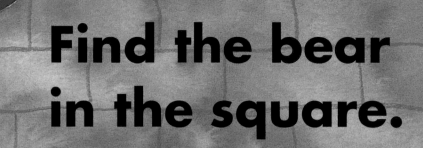

**Find the hearts
in the queen's hair.**

Find the circles in the pool.

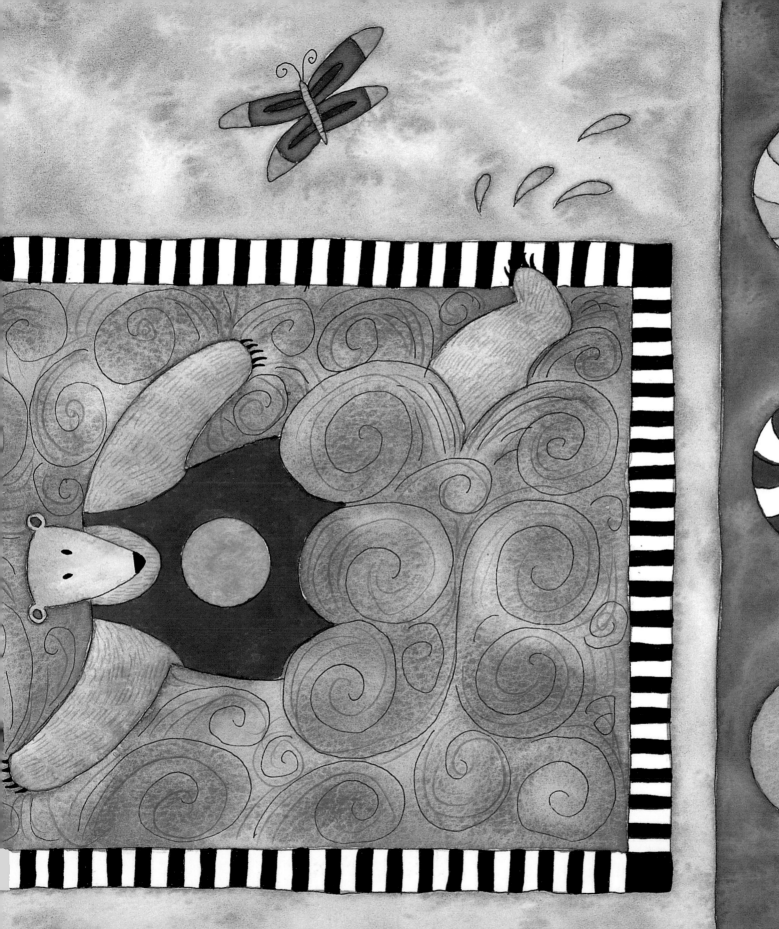

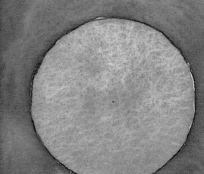

Find the rectangles in the school.

Find the moons in the cave.

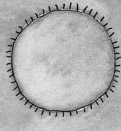

Find the triangles on the wave.

Find the diamonds on the crown.

Find the zigzags around the clown.

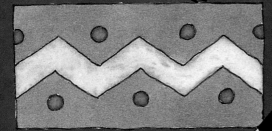

Find the ovals
in the park.

Find the stars in the dark.

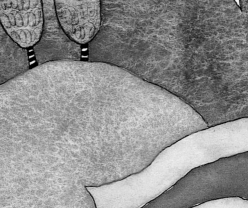

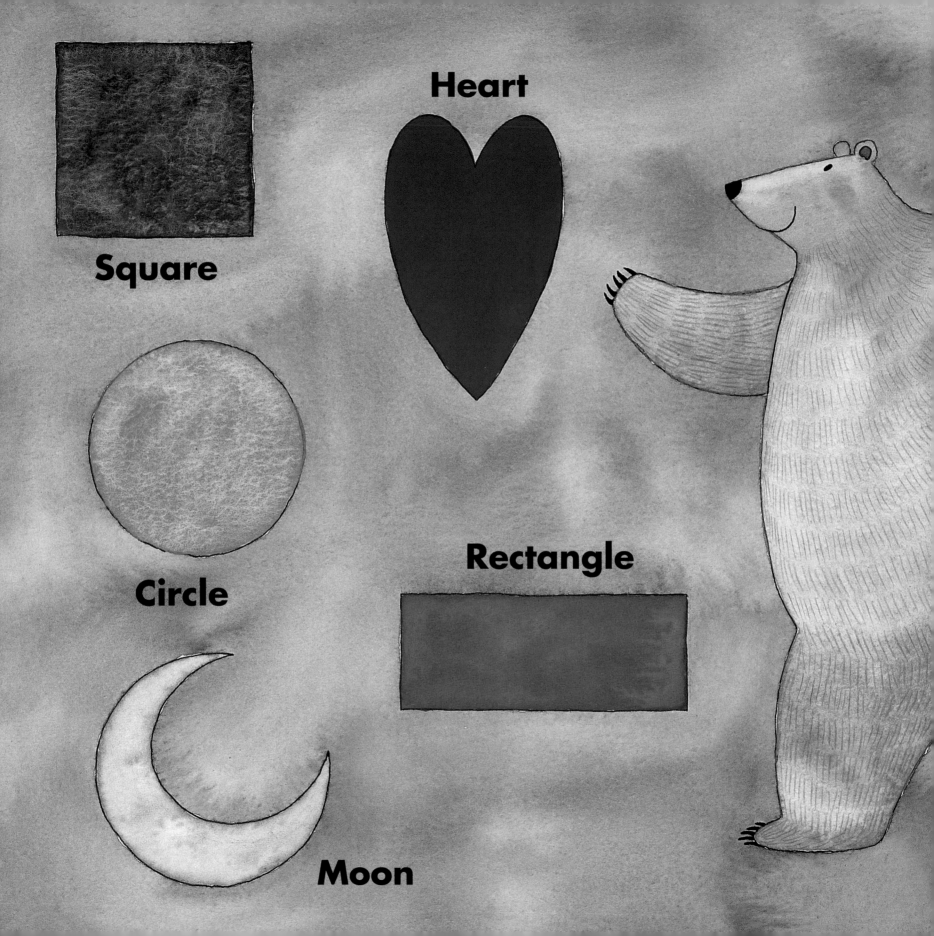

Square

Heart

Circle

Rectangle

Moon

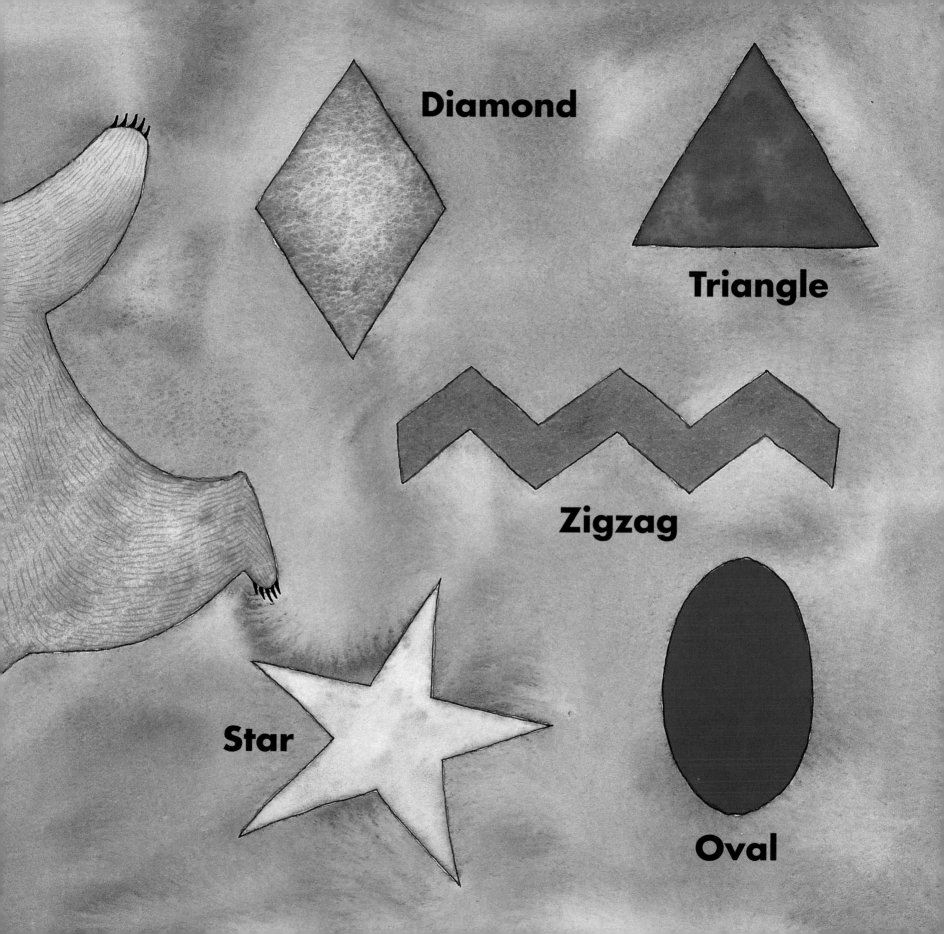

Diamond

Triangle

Zigzag

Star

Oval

For more fun with Bear:

BEAR ABOUT TOWN — Stella Blackstone • Debbie Harter • Henry Strozier

BEAR AT HOME — Stella Blackstone • Debbie Harter • Henry Strozier

BEAR AT WORK — Stella Blackstone • Debbie Harter • Henry Strozier

BEAR IN SUNSHINE — Stella Blackstone • Debbie Harter • Henry Strozier

BEAR ON A BIKE — Stella Blackstone • Debbie Harter • Henry Strozier

BEAR TAKES A TRIP — Stella Blackstone • Debbie Harter • Henry Strozier

BEAR'S BIRTHDAY — Stella Blackstone • Debbie Harter • Henry Strozier

BEAR'S BUSY FAMILY — Stella Blackstone • Debbie Harter • Henry Strozier

BEAR'S SCHOOL DAY — Stella Blackstone • Debbie Harter • Henry Strozier

Barefoot Books, 23 Bradford Street, 2nd Floor, Concord, MA 01742
Barefoot Books, 29/30 Fitzroy Square, London, W1T 6LQ

Text copyright © 1998 by Stella Blackstone
Illustrations copyright © 1998 by Debbie Harter
The moral rights of Stella Blackstone and Debbie Harter have been asserted

Audiobook narrated
by Henry Strozier
Recorded by
Lotas Studios,
New York City, USA
Sound Supervision
by Michael Flannery,
www.jumpinggiant.com

First published in the United States of America by Barefoot Books, Inc
and in Great Britain by Barefoot Books, Ltd in 1998
This paperback edition first published in 2021. All rights reserved

Graphic design by Jennie Hoare, England
Printed in China on 100% acid-free paper

This book was typeset in Slappy and Futura
The illustrations were prepared in paint, pen and ink, and crayon

Paperback ISBN 978-1-84686-055-3
Board book ISBN 978-1-84148-287-3
E-book ISBN 978-1-78285-944-4

British Cataloguing-in-Publication Data:
a catalogue record for this book is available from the British Library

Library of Congress Cataloging-in-Publication Data
is available under LCCN 2005018216

3 5 7 9 8 6 4 2

Go to **www.barefootbooks.com/bearsquare**
to access your audiobook online.